Written by Christy Webster
Illustrations by Kaley McCabe

All rights reserved. Published in the United States by Random House Children's Books,
a division of Penguin Random House LLC, New York.

Random House and the colophon are registered trademarks of Penguin Random House LLC.

Visit us on the Web!
rhcbooks.com

Educators and librarians, for a variety of teaching tools, visit us at RHTeachersLibrarians.com

Library of Congress Cataloging-in-Publication Data is available upon request.
ISBN 978-0-593-65175-9 (trade) — ISBN 978-0-593-65176-6 (lib. bdg.) — ISBN 978-0-593-65177-3 (ebook)

MANUFACTURED IN CHINA
10 9 8 7 6 5 4 3 2 1

Uni the UNICORN

Mermaid Helper

an Amy Krouse Rosenthal book
written by Christy Webster
pictures based on art by Brigette Barrager

Random House 🏠 New York

It was a perfect day for a walk by the seaside. Uni the unicorn was listening to the gentle waves crashing along the shore, when suddenly Uni's friend cried out.

The little girl had a lot of questions. The mermaid thought them over.

Uni knew exactly what to do. Soon the three of them were galloping away from the shore.

They showed the mermaid the view from Uni's favorite hillside.

Wow!

Then Uni and the little girl brought the mermaid to the magical forest where Uni lived. The other unicorns had never seen a mermaid before, and it made them shy.

I love climbing trees, but it's easier with help from a friend!

The little girl had an idea.

The mermaid was so grateful she clapped her hands with joy.

The mermaid thanked Uni and the little girl for the amazing trip on land, and swam back to her grotto.